AESOP AWESOME RHYMES

THE LION AND THE MOUSE

Written by **Lou Kuenzler**
Illustrated by **Jill Newton**

ORCHARD

Old Aesop was an Ancient Greek —
his AWESOME FABLES are unique.
Each fun tale gives good advice
reminding us we must be nice.

Do not drop litter in the street.
Always keep your bedroom neat.
Be polite to any guest.
When it's chilly, wear a vest!
You'll surely learn these simple rules
unless you are a bunch of fools!

Now read this fable, if you're wise.
See kindness bring a BIG surprise . . .

We meet a lion, fierce and bold.
His teeth are sharp, although he's old.
He'd often shoo the cubs away
and take a rest around midday.

The cubs cried, "Let's get out of here!
Don't wake him up. He'll bite your ear!"
Every animal always knows,
it's best to let a lion doze!

Leon (or 'lion' in Ancient Greece)
was king and ruled the jungle beasts.
But he's not the hero of this tale.
Our star's on a much smaller scale . . .

Our champ's a tiny mouse called Tim.
A real cutie – look at him!
Now, Tim was heading out to find
some nuts and seeds – things of that kind.
A little snack, around midday,
to chase his hunger pains away.

He wasn't focussed – not at all –
instead he thought about . . . FOOTBALL.
Mouse United were his side,
Tim wore his scarf with real pride.
He was due to see them play
against the Meerkat team that day.

As Tim dreamed they'd win the cup,
something suddenly tripped him up.
Unknown to Tim, old Leon's tail
was hidden by dust – all yellow and pale.

The mouse went flying through the air,
and landed SPLAT in Leon's hair.
"Who's that?" growled Leon, wide awake.
"To rouse me was a BIG mistake!"

Poor Tim clung silent as he could.
But trying to hide did him no good.

The lion ROARED and shook his mane
and Tim flew through the air again.
He landed right by Leon's paws –
the lion grabbed him in his claws.

"But Sire," squealed Tim. "I'm very small.
I will not fill you up at all!"
"QUIET!" growled Leon, "You were
   unwise
to wake me rudely, by surprise.

I dreamed a lovely lion dream,
about my beautiful lioness queen.
We strolled together, paw in paw,
and danced along the moonlit shore."

"S-sounds romantic!" stuttered Tim.
But angry Leon roared at him:

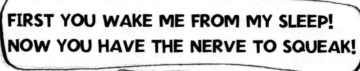

FIRST YOU WAKE ME FROM MY SLEEP!
NOW YOU HAVE THE NERVE TO SQUEAK!

The lion opened his mouth WIDE,
about to pop poor Tim inside . . .

"Please!" begged Tim. "Your Royal
  Highness,
let's make a deal. Please show some
  kindness!"
"A deal?" Leon asked, and swung
  Tim's scarf.
"Really, Titch! Don't make me laugh."

"Listen!" said Tim. "Here's an idea:
Free me now. But I'll stay near.
If ever you're in any trouble,
I'll come running on the double!"

"YOU help ME?" Leon roared with
  laughter,
"I've NEVER heard of anything
  DAFTER!
How can a little mousey thing
help me, a mighty lion king?
Oh, what a VERY funny joke,"
Leon was grinning as he spoke.

"You've really made me smile today
So I will let you get away.
My tiny pal, you're far too funny
to end your life inside my tummy.
Run along! Don't even squeak!
NEVER again wake me from sleep!"

There was no need to tell Tim twice.
He sped away – gone in a trice.

"I'll keep my promise," he called, and ran.
"I'll help you out, if ever I can.
To set me free was a kindly thing.
A gentle act, my noble king!"

That afternoon by kick-off time,
Tim had recovered –

He told his friends, who waved blue
scarves,
how he'd escaped. The mice all laughed.

"You never know," Tim tried to say.
But then the whistle started play!

The cheering mice waved tails and paws.
They squeaked and shouted, whooped
and ROARED!

Mice never lose! We never draw!
We are the tiny team who score!

You Meerkats should stay in your holes
You're just no good at scoring goals!

The grotty pitch was quite run-down.
But that did not make young Tim frown.

While little Tim cheered his team on,
King Leon's day went very wrong.
He found another spot to nap,
but sprung the spring on a hunter's trap.
A net fell down from high above.
It held his body like a glove!

As Leon struggled, the net pulled tight.
There was no way the lion could fight.
He roared with all his massive lungs:

Tim heard the shouting from the stands
He knew that he must change his plans.

I can't stay here and watch the game
while I know the king's in pain.
The match is gripping – drawn one all!
But I promised help, if he should call.

The lion was tied inside the net,
tangled, twisted, dripping sweat.
As Tim came near, Leon hung his head,
"I suppose you've come to laugh?" he
said.

"Of course not – I've not come to grin.
I've come to help you!" explained Tim.
"I came because I heard your roar.
So just stay still and let me gnaw."

Tim took the net between his teeth,
chewing quickly underneath.

Careful where you're nibbling, chum!
I don't want tooth marks on my bum!

With small, sharp bites Tim cut the cords
until, at last, the lion roared,
"I'm free, you clever little thing!
A tiny mouse has saved the king!"

"Jump on my back!" King Leon
    laughed.
"We'll make it for the second half!"

Let's grab some net before we dash –
I've an idea to help the match!

As Leon raced towards the game,
our Tim clung tightly to his mane.

True to his word, Leon returned Tim
to see the second half begin.
A last minute goal – Mouse United
    scored!
Tim, his friends, and the lion

ROARED!

While Tim perched high on Leon's head,
the lion shouted up and said,
"Mouse United won the match
but their score was not a patch
on yours, my tiny little friend.
You saved me from a knotty end!
The hunters put me in the net,
but you turned up to pay your debt.
I'm certain now, that I'd be dead,
without the sharp teeth in your head."

Tim said, "No worries!" then jumped down
and grabbed their net up from the ground.

Just lend a paw before you go.
That's all the thanks I need, you know.

They stretched the net behind the goals,
and tied it tightly to the poles.

The pitch looked smart now at both ends.
And Tim and Leon were best of friends.

45

So, here's the moral we have learned:
A kindly act will be returned.
However BIG and strong you seem,
it makes good sense to form a team.
Kindness goes a long, long way –
it just might save your life one day!

AESOP'S AWESOME RHYMES

Written by Lou Kuenzler
Illustrated by Jill Newton

All priced at £4.99

Orchard Books are available
from all good bookshops, or can
be ordered from our website,
www.orchardbooks.co.uk,
or telephone 01235 827702,
or fax 01235 827703.